Actually, it was Badger who did the pedalling, while Hare sang a range of popular songs "to keep old Badger going". He was also composing a Journey Song*, as he called it. He tried out the first few verses.

*Text opposite title page.

HARE AND BADGER GO TO TOWN

By Naomi Lewis & Tony Ross

ANDERSEN PRESS · LONDON
HUTCHINSON OF AUSTRALIA

First published in Great Britain in 1981 by Andersen Press Ltd., London, W1.
Published in Australia by Hutchinson Group (Australia) Pty. Ltd., Victoria 3121.
Text © 1981 by Naomi Lewis. Illustrations © 1981 by Tony Ross.
Printed in Italy by Grafiche AZ, Verona. ISBN 0 905478 94 0.

ZOOM!

Hare and Badger woke with a start.

No—not again!

But it *was* happening again. The aeroplane full of chemicals was zooming over the barley field; once again, everything was covered with poisonous dust. This time they would *have* to move. NOW.

They packed a few treasures, took a last sad look at their house in the willow bank, mounted their two-seater bicycle, and off they rode.

Goodbye, little home!

By nightfall, they were glad to rest. They sheltered under an overturned cardboard box in a field, and soon fell fast asleep.

ZZZZZZZZZZZZZ, BONK!

Hare and Badger bolted upright. The air smelt like morning. Whatever had woken them? It *looked* like a bee, but—

—it was wearing a kind of mask!

"Bee," said Hare. "I hope you don't mind me asking, but is that the fashion round here? I mean that thing on your face."

"It's my gas-mask," mumbled the bee. "To keep out all that chemical dust. It gets into everything. My honey tastes so awful, my family won't eat it." He was blundering about as he spoke, knocking against the flowers.

"That's why *we* left home," said Hare. "Now, you see the world as you fly around; which way do you advise us to go?"

"Which way have you come from?"

Badger pointed back.

"Then I should go as far in the opposite direction as you can," said the bee. "Even if it leads to the city. Not that I've been there myself."

"That's just what we'll do," said Hare.

The sun was high overhead when they stopped. They had to! They had reached a stream, and there wasn't a bridge or boat in sight.

But they weren't alone. A kingfisher sat on a twig, trying to fish with a rod and line. Round her beak was a handkerchief. What a peculiar sight! "Yes, I know I look odd," she said, removing the handkerchief. "But I wear it to keep out the smell. The water's terrible! Full of pollution. Puh!"

She replaced the handkerchief.

"Can you tell us," said Badger, "why the fields are so quiet and empty—not a pig, not a hen, not a calf in sight for miles?"

Kingfisher took off the handkerchief again.

"Don't you know anything?" she said.
"Humans keep those poor animals jammed
together in terrible prisons; they never come out
alive. Factory farms—that's what the prisons are
called. You'll know you are near by the smell;
it's worse than this! Sorry, that's all for now."
She replaced the handkerchief.

Hare and Badger went along the bank,
wondering how to cross. "What did she say was
wrong with the water?" asked Badger, peering
down.

"Bubble, bubble, bubble, I can tell you," said a
voice. A huge fish was looking up at them. On
his back was a kind of bottle with a rubber tube
leading into his mouth. "Clever, isn't it!" said

the fish. "This river was once a fine place to live in, lovely sparkling water—a real treat! Now those humans pour in horrible stuff from factories. Soon there won't be any fish left. It's horribubble, bubble."

"I'm ever so sorry," said Badger. "It's almost as bad up here. That's why we're on the move. But we don't know how to cross the stream."

"Oh, I'll take you over," said the genial fish. "But I can't manage the bike."

"That's all right," said Badger quickly. He was quite worn out with pedalling. "You're welcome to use it—spare tubes or anything." He waved an airy paw.

They climbed on to the fish's back, and sped to the opposite bank.

"Many thanks," called Hare. "We'll remember
that good turn."

The fish waved its fin. "Don't mention it. By
the way, if you're not sure where to go next, you
might try over the hill. I've seen quite a few
animals going that way. Though no one has
ever told me what's on the other side."

They reached the top of the hill at last, and stood amazed. Down below they saw hundreds of buildings, closely packed together; lights twinkled everywhere.

"It's a city!" cried Hare. "The one we were singing about. Come on!"

In the gathering darkness they scampered towards the unknown.

But was this the longed-for place? Hare and Badger held paws as they wandered from street to street, feeling lost and bewildered. The ground was hard—not a single tuft of grass. When they looked up, tall buildings blotted out most of the sky. And among other noises were regular sounds that never stopped: zim, zim, clankety clank—the tireless voice of machines.

ROS 14S

Suddenly, a blinding light flashed round the
corner and a huge red monster thundered
towards them. Where could they hide? What
about that round hole in the road with an iron
lid beside it?

A moment later they had leapt down into the
dark.

Bump! Bump!

They landed on a kind of ledge, and crouched there till daylight. Perhaps some dreadful chasm lay below! But quite soon they heard a voice.

"Hoy! You up there! Step down. It isn't far."

Now they could just see a black stream gurgling away below. In a little boat that bobbed up and down was a water-rat. It was he who had called them; now he helped them aboard, and they glided off. Other small craft were drifting about in the gloom.

"Country folk, eh?" said the water-rat. "You're not the only ones; they come in every day." He steered the boat to a jetty with small stone steps. At the top, a line of light shone from under a door. A painted sign above said "The Pig and Trumpet."

"Just go in there," said the rat, "and ask for Fox."

Timidly, Hare and Badger opened the door.
Surprise! In the hot bright room before them
animals sprawled about everywhere, laughing
and singing, a glass in every hand. Some were
playing cards. At the far end of the room a
wise-looking fox stood behind a counter covered
with bottles of dandelion wine. He gave the
newcomers a welcoming nod, and in no time at
all Hare and Badger were pouring out their tale
to him as he poured out the beer.

"I know," he said. "It's the same with us all.
Humans are the trouble, of course. They've
poisoned and destroyed so much of the
countryside that some animals think that the
only safe place left is where humans live

themselves—in towns. In fact, the animals here
have built a little city of their own, modelled on
the human one overhead. We're in it now! Wait
until closing time; you can stay the night with
me and I'll tell you more."

At last the animals started to leave, dancing and singing, very much out of tune. Hare and Badger stood at the door, watching them disappear into streets and blocks of flats very much like the human ones above.

Fox soon joined them and took them home, where they sat round the fire and talked. "Everyone *seems* happy here," said Badger. "Are they all really happy?"

"It's a case of yes and no," said Fox. "When you copy human comforts, you have to copy more than you expect. Animal City is setting up factories too; it has even begun to build on the

few green patches about the town too small or
inconvenient for humans to bother about. Still,
tomorrow we'll go sightseeing. You seem an
intelligent pair; you can tell me then what you
think."

As soon as breakfast was over, Fox and his
guests set off. The underground city was
teeming with early animals, as a cold light
streamed from the iron gratings above. They
were all on their way to work. "Comforts don't
come for nothing," murmured Fox. "The
factories have to keep going." As they passed
shops and chip-stalls, and even amusement
arcades, Hare and Badger felt quite dazed; their
willow bank seemed very far away. Suddenly Fox
stopped, at a white door with a red cross
painted on it. "A hospital," he said. "You need
them in a city."

One of the many patients caught their
attention—a fieldmouse, covered with bandages.

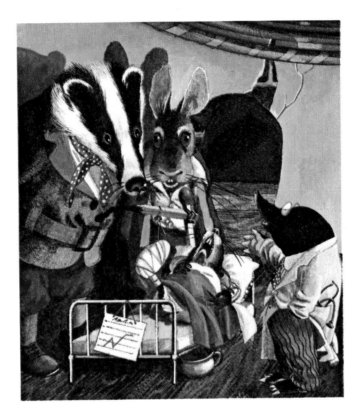

Hare and Badger recognised him—he came
from their own wood. "Sad case," murmured
Doctor Mole, who seemed to know Fox well.
"Chemical burns. Factories, you know. We get
plenty of those."

They went out into the street.

"What do animals want with factories?"
Badger said. He had been silent most of the
morning. "Humans have nothing to teach us.
We have gifts and skills that they can never
match. Besides, we're quiet and orderly; we leave
no mess; we bring up our children properly. We
don't eat humans; we don't use them as they use
us, and we don't need their nasty inventions."

That was quite a speech for him, and he
blushed to see that a crowd was gathering. They
made approving noises.

"If we stay here long we'll forget what *we* can
do," cried Hare. "I mean run, and leap, and
sense danger, and find our way in the dark. I
vote we pull down the animal factories."

"We're with you, mate," said a number of
animal voices. The crowd had grown.

"When we've done," Hare went on, "we'll
find small places around where humans
wouldn't expect us; we'll make our own secret
woods and fields where the chemical sprays
can't reach. Come on!"

On they came; they didn't need human tools
to do their work. As they advanced on the pipes
and wires they joined in the Journey Song. Hare

had written a special extra section; it didn't take
long to learn.

Towns are not for us.
What can humans teach us?
Humans, they use us;
We don't use human creatures.

Night came. Yes—it had been a glorious day.
At last no machines were left in Animal City,
and the mess had been cleared into piles.

"Tomorrow," said Hare, "we must plant grass and seeds and flowers. Some might come up through the chimneys—I'd like that effect."

Hare and Badger lay down where they were, and fell fast asleep, just as if they were in their old home....

ZOOM! They woke with a start. Had it all been a dream?

They *were* in their old home.

And the aeroplane was overhead again.

They would really have to leave, and find a new place NOW.

But at least they had some new ideas on the matter...